Disney
CLUB PENGUIN™

Before *Card-Jitsu:*
The Ninja Quest

Disney CLUB PENGUIN™

Before *Card-Jitsu:* The Ninja Quest

PICK YOUR PATH 6

by Tracey West

Published by Ladybird Books Ltd 2012
A Penguin Company

Penguin Books Ltd, 80 Strand,
London, WC2R ORL, UK
Penguin Books Australia Ltd,
Camberwell, Victoria, Australia
Penguin Group (NZ), 67 Apollo Drive, Rosedale,
Auckland 0632, New Zealand
(a division of Pearson New Zealand Ltd)

ISBN: 9781409391005
Printed in Great Britain
001 - 10 9 8 7 6 5 4 3 2 1

Some time ago, before the Dojo was built . . .

The snow crunches underneath your flippers as you wander through the wilds of Club Penguin. You're on an adventure, and you're prepared for anything: Your warm coat and boots will protect you from the elements; your helmet will keep you from harm; and you've got a rope, food and water in your rucksack.

The only thing you're missing is a map showing exactly where you need to go. That's because you don't really know where you're going. The reason you've embarked on this quest is because of a mysterious rumour you've heard.

It started with whispers about ninjas, black-clad penguins expert in the art of mastering the elements. You've never seen one, but other penguins swear they've seen signs that the ninjas exist. The latest rumour is that a mysterious grey penguin with a white beard and a wide straw hat has been spotted in the wilderness. They say he looks like a wise ninja master.

Most penguins are content to just talk about the ninjas, but you have the heart of an adventurer. That's why, days ago, you set out to find this ninja master. But all you've found so far is snow, snow and more snow. The only thing you've noticed that's unusual is the sky over Club Penguin, which is streaked with orange. But that has nothing to do with the ninjas—or does it?

"I wonder if I should turn back," you say out loud. The thought makes you sad. You don't want your adventure to be over so soon.

You sit down on a rock, trying to decide what to do. That's when you notice a plume of smoke rising from a circle of pine trees in the distance.

"That's curious," you remark. "Maybe my adventure isn't over yet."

You hoist your rucksack on your shoulders and trek toward the smoke. As you quietly step into the circle of trees, you are amazed to see a grey penguin sitting at the edge of a small, reflective pond. A small fire burns next to him, and a teapot is hanging over the fire, supported by a stand made from tree branches.

Your heart starts to beat faster. The penguin has a long, white beard, bushy, white eyebrows, and wears a straw hat on his head. Is this the mysterious ninja master you have been searching for?

"Come closer, my friend."

The penguin's voice startles you. His back is turned to you, and you wonder how he knows you are there.

"Hello," you say, waddling up to the pond. You tell the penguin your name.

"It is a pleasure to meet you," he replies, turning to you. "You may call me Sensei."

"That means *teacher*, doesn't it?" you ask. You did some reading up on ninjas before your journey.

Sensei nods. "It does indeed," he replies. "You appear to be clever, young penguin. And bold. No other penguin has ever ventured so far into the wilderness."

"I heard a rumour that there was a ninja master somewhere on the island," you tell him. "I would love to train to be a ninja. So I set out on a quest . . . and I found you."

Sensei is silent for a moment. Finally, he speaks:

"I have been searching for a penguin to help me with a very important task," he says. "Will you assist me?"

Your heart starts to beat quickly. This is exactly the adventure you were hoping for!

"Of course I'll help you!" you reply. "What do you need me to do?"

Sensei takes the teapot off the fire and pours two cups of tea. Then he pats the ground next to him, motioning for you to sit. When you do, he hands you a cup of tea. It's warm and smells delicious.

"I know there are many penguins on the island who want to become ninjas," Sensei begins. "To train so many ninjas will be a difficult task—but not impossible. To do that, I must build a Dojo so penguins can learn the ways of the ninja."

"That's like a training gym, right?" you ask.

Sensei nods. "In the Dojo, I can instruct penguins in the art of mastering the elements."

You're puzzled. "Mastering the elements?"

"Fire, snow and water," Sensei explains. "Each has a different power. Each can be dangerous if not controlled. But when they are mastered, great things can happen."

"So you need me to help build the Dojo?" you ask.

"Before the Dojo can be built, the perfect location must be found," Sensei responds. "It must be a place where fire, water and snow come together in harmony."

Sensei unrolls a paper scroll, and you see a map of Club Penguin on it. It's not like the map you normally use—it shows all of the island's natural features, including mountains, rivers and caves.

"I created this map during my travels," he says. "You can use it as you search for the best place for the Dojo."

Then he hands you something else—a small book with a black cover. The title simply reads *Haiku*.

"A haiku is a special kind of poem," he says. "The verses in this book may help you when you are in trouble or unsure of your path."

You open the book to a random page. This is the verse you see:

"Alone you travel.
But when a friend offers help,
Do not refuse her."

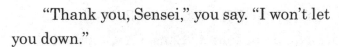

"Thank you, Sensei," you say. "I won't let you down."

Sensei stands up. "Study the map," he tells you. "You must decide where you will go."

Sensei walks off into the trees. You look at the map, trying to find a place where fire, snow and water all meet. There is snow everywhere, of course, so you decide to narrow your search. There are two things that stand out.

One is a river that snakes across Club Penguin. You didn't even know it existed. That makes water and snow—but no fire.

The other is a hot spring—that's fire and water together, but it's underground, so there's no snow. You'll have to explore to be sure, but which place will you explore first?

If you explore the river first, go to page 31.

If you explore the underground spring, go to page 47.

Sensei is very pleased with the tea that you bring him. He opens up a wood box and brings out a tea set with a blue teapot and four matching cups on a round tray.

"Since you appreciate tea, you may enjoy this," he says, giving it to you.

"Thanks, Sensei!" you say. You take out the map. "I guess now we have to get back to our search. We were trying to take the path around the mountain, but Jim says it's blocked."

"You must climb the mountain," Sensei says. "Only then can you decide what to do."

You nod. "We'll go back to the wide mountain and climb it. Thanks, Sensei!"

You all say your good-byes and then head back to the mountain, making a quick stop at your igloo to drop off the tea set. Refreshed, you start your journey once more.

Before long, you and Amy are back at the wide mountain, ready to climb.

Go to page 38.

CONTINUED FROM PAGE 26.

"Everyone believes you're real," you tell Pia. "If you go out there now and tell everyone about your prank, you'll be famous."

Pia looks thoughtful. "Okay," she says. "Lead the way."

You leave the Mine and jump out of the cart. "Hey, everybody!" you announce. "I found the ghost! Only it's not a ghost at all. It's a penguin in a sheet."

The penguins look confused. You look behind you and there's no sign of Pia. She's tricked you.

You frown. "Okay, maybe I can't prove I saw the ghost," you say. "But I met Sensei, a ninja master, in the woods. He gave me this map."

You get the map from your pack—and it's blank!

"Honestly, this used to be a map," you say.

The other penguins don't seem to believe you. Have you been imagining things?

THE END

CONTINUED FROM PAGE 40.

Using the rope might be easier than going back and getting the ladders.

"Let's try the rope," you say, getting the rope and grappling hook out of your pack.

"Throw it to the other side and then hold on to the other end," Amy suggests. "Then, after I climb to the other side, I'll throw the hook back to you and it's your turn."

You twirl the grappling hook above your head. "All right, let's do this!"

You throw the hook to the other side of the ravine and the metal hooks clamp firmly into the frozen ground. The rope stretches across the ravine and you wrap the other end around your waist and grab the end. You give it a yank and it holds steady.

"We're good to go," you say.

Amy takes a deep breath and grabs on to the rope, pulling herself over the ravine. She doesn't get far when the grappling hook starts to strain from the weight of her and her heavy pack.

"Amy, come back!" you yell.

But before she can, the grappling hook comes

loose and slides across the ice. The rope dangles into the ravine, swinging Amy from side to side.

Panicked, you steady yourself so you won't get pulled into the ravine, too. Then you pull up on the rope with all your might. Amy falls on her back, exhausted and terrified. "You saved me," she says. "I can't thank you enough."

You're both really shaken up. This is dangerous! You go back to Sensei and tell him what you've found.

"So this middle mountain is actually a volcano," you say, showing him the map. "I've marked it for you. I don't know if there is water nearby, but there's definitely fire and ice."

Sensei nods. "You have done well," he says. "I am closer to building the Dojo than ever before. And when ninja training finally begins, both of you will be ready."

He hands each of you a white ninja robe with a white belt.

"It is called a *gi*," he explains. "Wear it, and others will know you are ninjas-in-training."

"Cool!" you and Amy say.

THE END

CONTINUED FROM PAGE 32.

A motorboat might make your journey faster, but something tells you that it's better to take things slow and pay attention. You decide to walk along the riverbank instead.

It's a beautiful day, and you feel full of new energy since you met Sensei. As you walk, you keep your eyes open for any sign of a fire element, although you're not sure what that could be. A volcano maybe? But you've never heard of a volcano on Club Penguin.

Soon you start to get hungry, and you remember that your food supplies are low. Then you spot a cluster of O'berry bushes in the distance and give a happy shout.

"Oh yeah!" O'berries are o-shaped berries that grow in the wild. Puffles love them, but penguins can eat them, too, even though they're very spicy and bitter. But when you're out in the wilderness, it's better than not having any food at all. You decide to stock up.

You fill your rucksack with the berries and then sit down for a snack. As you're munching on them, you notice something moving on the riverbank, in the direction you just came from. You squint against the sunlight to get a better look. It's a black puffle!

It's always exciting to see a puffle in the wild. You'd love to make contact, but you know you'll have to be careful—wild puffles can be very shy. You're about to go after the puffle when you stop yourself. You're in the middle of an important job. Should you stay focused on your task?

If you befriend the puffle, go to page 36.

If you keep going, go to page 74.

CONTINUED FROM PAGE 30.

Sharing the treasure with the other penguins is an opportunity you don't want to miss. Now you just have to figure out how to get the treasure out of the Mine. There's no way you'll be able to lift up the treasure chest to get it through that hole in the wall.

You end up dumping flipperfuls of jewels through the hole. Then you load a mine cart with the treasure and ride it out of the Mine. When you emerge into the sunshine, the gathered penguins gasp.

"Is that treasure?" someone asks.

"Yes, it is!" you say happily. "Follow me to the Town. There's enough for everybody!"

When you arrive in the crowded Town Centre, curious penguins gather around you.

"Come get your treasure here!" you announce. "One piece per penguin, please!"

The penguins cheer, and you feel like a real hero as they line up to choose a piece of the treasure. You reach in and grab a glittering, gold crown and put it on your head. Right now, you feel just like a king or queen.

"What'll it be?" you ask the penguins as they come up. "A gold coin? A ruby bracelet? An emerald paperweight?"

> "Gold can make you rich.
> But staying on the true path?
> More precious than gold."

You look up and see Sensei in front of you!

"Hi, Sensei," you say. "I found this treasure, but I plan to keep on looking for the Dojo when I'm done."

Sensei doesn't say anything. He simply nods his head and disappears into the crowd. You keep giving out treasure until everyone has some. The penguins take you out for pizza to celebrate.

Much later, you remember your quest for the Dojo. You reach into your rucksack to find the map—but it's gone.

Sensei's words come back to you, and you realise you've lost your chance to help him. Maybe you shouldn't have taken the treasure— but at least you made a lot of penguins happy!

THE END

CONTINUED FROM PAGE 70.

"I'm sorry, Amy," you say. "I think I need to do this alone."

"I understand," your friend says. "Just be careful, okay?"

You nod. "Of course!" you promise.

After buying the equipment you need, you head off to follow the path you found on the map. It's a beautiful day, and you have a good feeling that you're heading in the right direction.

You make up a silly song as you go.

"The Sensei's gonna build a Doooooojooo!"

There's no one around to hear you, so you sing as loud as you can. You raise your voice to the tall mountain peaks that surround you.

"The Dojo, the Dooojooooo!"

A sound like thunder rumbles in the valley, and you see a wall of snow rushing down the nearest mountainside. It's an avalanche!

You've got to get to safety, fast! Desperately, you look around for a place to avoid the frozen wave that's headed your way. Then you spot a cave entrance up ahead, and you run as fast as your flippers can carry you.

19

You reach the cave just as the wall of snow descends from the mountain and piles up on the ground right outside. The massive pile of snow blocks the entrance to the cave. You're trapped!

"Heeeeelp!" you cry.

You try to dig your way out with your grappling hook but it's a slow, hard task. Hours pass until, suddenly, part of the wall begins to melt in front of you. A glowing orange light shines through the snow. What's going on?

Sensei steps through a hole in the snow, carrying a flaming torch.

"Sensei, I am so glad to see you!" you say gratefully. "Thank you for rescuing me."

"Thank the power of the elements," he says, nodding at the torch.

"I guess my quest is over," you say.

"Perhaps not," Sensei says. "I should not have sent you out without teaching you how to master the elements. If you agree to be my student, I will teach you what I know. Then you may begin your search again."

"It would be an honour to be your student," you say, bowing to Sensei.

THE END

CONTINUED FROM PAGE 68.

Sliding across the ice sounds like fun, but you're not sure if it's safe.

"Let's stay on land just to be sure," you tell the black puffle, and it nods in agreement.

As you walk on, you notice that the ice on the river is very thin and breaking in parts, so you know that you made the right decision. But you're starting to wish that your search wasn't taking you so long. You've come all this way, and the only sign of fire you've seen has been the black puffle.

You keep going, and soon you come to another mountain. A waterfall flows straight down the side. The water is a beautiful shade of blue, and you're struck by the sight. It's snow and water in perfect harmony. But there's still no sign of fire.

Discouraged, you find a rock, sit down and look at the map. Just past this mountain, the river runs to the sea.

"What now?" you wonder out loud.

Then you remember the book of haiku that Sensei gave you. He said that the verses could help you when you didn't know what to do. You decide to give it a try.

You take the book out of your pack and open it to a random page. The black puffle looks over your shoulder, curious.

"Maybe I should let you pick the page for me," you say.

If you let the puffle open the book, go to page 43.

If you open the book, go to page 63.

CONTINUED FROM PAGE 55.

"Let's just drop down to the ledge," you suggest. "I'm anxious to keep going."

You attach your grappling hook firmly to the top of the ledge and dangle the rope down to the bottom.

"Be careful," Amy warns as you shimmy down.

The drop to the ledge is longer than you thought. The rope doesn't quite reach the bottom, so you have to jump to reach your shoe. When you hop off, you stumble and roll across the ledge, knocking off your boot. You try to stop yourself, but you nearly tumble off the ledge! You grip a nearby rock and try to pull yourself back up.

To your relief you see Amy standing above you. She holds out her flipper.

"I'll pull you up!" she tells you.

As Amy hoists you up, your rucksack slides off your shoulders. Your instinct is to save it, but then you risk falling over the side again. Safely on your feet, you watch the pack crash onto the rocks below.

Amy hugs you. "I'm so glad you're okay!"

"Thanks for coming to get me," you reply. "I don't know what I would do without you."

23

Amy turns to show you her back—and her pack is gone, too. "I lost it when I slid down the rope to get you. I was in a hurry and wasn't being careful."

You sigh. "We can't go on without our equipment. We'll have to go back to the Gift Shop and get more supplies."

Amy agrees that it's the best thing to do. You go back to the Gift Shop and restock.

You follow the path back to the wide mountain. But when you get to the top and look at the mountains in the distance, you don't see the volcano.

"That's so weird," Amy remarks. "All of the mountains are snowy. And there's no smoke."

"Maybe we're on top of the wrong wide mountain," you say nervously. "I don't know. We've done our best, but maybe the place Sensei is looking for just doesn't exist."

THE END

CONTINUED FROM PAGE 48.

You decide to throw some snowballs and see what happens. You whip two toward the direction of the noise you heard and wait.

Everything's quiet for a few seconds. Then . . . s*plat! Splat! Splat! Splat! Splat!*

A whole bunch of snowballs comes flying through the tunnel at you. You duck and the snowballs harmlessly hit the walls. But now you're more curious than ever.

You run toward the snowballs and are startled to see a ghost standing in front of you! At least, you think it's a ghost at first. But then you quickly realise it's just a penguin wearing a sheet.

"Nice costume," you say. "What are you doing in here?"

"This is noooooot a costuuuuuume," the penguin replies in a spooky voice. "I'm a ghooooooooost!"

"Well, you look like a penguin in a sheet," you say.

The penguin sighs and pulls off the white sheet she's wearing. You were right! Underneath she's just a regular purple penguin.

"Guess you caught me," she says. "But please don't tell anyone, okay?"

You're confused. "I don't get it. Why are you pretending to be a ghost?"

"My name's Pia. My friends are always pranking me," she explains. "I've been looking for a way to get them back. Then I heard the rumours about the ghost and I thought I would have a little fun."

"Everyone out there is pretty scared," you say. "Maybe you should come out with me and tell them the truth."

"But I'm just getting started!" Pia protests. She looks thoughtful for a moment. "Hey, I've got an idea. With your help, I can play the greatest ghostly prank ever. We'll be famous!"

Pia's offer is tempting. You love a good prank.

If you convince Pia to go with you, go to page 12.

If you agree to help her with her prank, go to page 73.

CONTINUED FROM PAGE 55.

"Let's take the path," you say. "It's steep, but it's probably safer than dropping down to the ledge with a rope."

The two of you make your way down the steep trail. It's not easy because you've only got one boot and with every step you risk losing control and sliding down the path. But you make it safely to the ledge.

You put on the boot, and then you and Amy carefully make your way up the side of the volcano. You reach the volcano's peak without any more trouble.

"So the volcano represents fire, and there's snow all around," you say. "Now we just need to find some water."

"You mean like that waterfall over there?" Amy asks, pointing.

You turn and see a blue waterfall flowing down the mountain right next to the volcano.

"This is it!" you cry. "The waterfall is water. It's the perfect spot for Sensei's Dojo!"

You and Amy high-five. Then you take out the map and mark everything you see so that

27

Sensei will be able to find it. Even better, from your spot on the volcano you can see a shortcut back to the main area of Club Penguin. You mark that path on the map, too.

Happy and excited, you and Amy hurry back to tell Sensei the good news. He's just as happy to see you.

"This is wonderful," Sensei says as he studies the map. "You have found the perfect location. Good work, young penguins. You have the heart and spirit of the ninja."

Sensei waddles over to a wooden chest and comes back with two white robes and white belts.

"This robe is called a *gi*, and it is worn by ninjas-in-training," he says. "I have one for each of you. The white belt shows that you have begun your first level."

"So when can we start training to be real ninjas?" you ask.

"First, I must build the Dojo," Sensei replies.

"But that could take a really long time," Amy points out.

"Yes, can't you please teach us now?" you ask. "We could help you build the Dojo while we're training."

Sensei smiles. "Your eagerness is pleasing. But you must have patience. I have been alone for a very long time, and I must have time to think when I build my Dojo."

You and Amy both look sad, and Sensei notices.

"However, you both show great promise," he says. "Let us do this. If you can answer my riddle, I will take you on as my pupils right away. If not, you must wait until the Dojo is built."

"We'll do it!" you and Amy say together.

"Here is the riddle," Sensei says. "You are the brother of the penguin standing next to you. But the penguin standing next to you is not your brother. How is that possible?"

If you answer, "Because the penguin is my sister," go to page 35.

If you answer, "Because the penguin is my cousin," go to page 60.

CONTINUED FROM PAGE 72.

You take the path to the left and see another dead end up ahead. You're about to turn back when something glints off your torch beam.

Curious, you move toward it. It's an old wooden chest that's filled with glittering jewels and coins! You can't believe your luck. You're rich!

You start to think of all the items you can buy, and then you think of something else—how cool would it be to share this with other penguins? You can bring the chest into Town and let everyone take something.

Then you remember—you're on a quest for Sensei. You can't stop now, can you?

If you take the treasure, go to page 17.

If you go back and take the path on the right, go to page 61.

CONTINUED FROM PAGES 10, 41.

"Sensei, I've made my decision," you announce.

The ninja master walks toward you.

"Where will you travel, young penguin?" he asks you.

You point to the map. "I'm going to head to the river," you tell him. "Water and snow meet on the riverbank. I'll travel along it until I find the third element, fire."

Sensei nods. "The choice is yours. I hope you find what you seek."

You hoist the pack onto your back once more. "I will do my best, Sensei," you promise. Then you head off in the direction of the river.

There's excitement in every step as you make your way across the snow-covered paths. You don't want to let Sensei down.

It takes more than an hour to reach the river on the map. Water rushes past you, and it's so clear and clean that you can see the rocks on the river floor underneath. You check the map and see that the current—the direction the water is flowing—leads right out to the sea, and you're not far from shore. That's probably not the best way to go. You're more interested in the path of the river that winds through the mountains. You think you'll have a better chance of finding some undiscovered fire element there.

On the map, the river looks very long. You can walk alongside on foot, but using a motorboat will be a lot faster. You know you can get a boat down at the Dock, but that will take you way out of your way. Is it worth it?

If you walk along the river, go to page 15.

If you go to the Dock and get a boat, go to page 50.

CONTINUED FROM PAGE 62.

You decide that blasting a hole through the ceiling will be the easiest thing to do. You head back the way you came and find the room with the cream soda barrels. First, you roll one barrel through the tunnels until you get to the hot spring.

It's hard work, and you're puffing and panting by the time you reach the spring. But you need one more barrel for your plan to work. You go get one more barrel and stop about ten feet away from the hot spring. Then you push as hard as you can, rolling the barrel faster and faster . . . and then you let go.

Smack! The second barrel crashes into the first barrel, which slams into the hard rock wall.

Boom! Both barrels explode, sending cream soda splashing everywhere.

You look up and see a small hole in the ceiling. Not bad! Maybe you can make the hole bigger with one more blast.

As you move to get two more barrels, the tunnel starts to shake and rumble around you. You fall to the ground and tumble across the floor, nearly sliding into the hot spring.

That was a close one! You slowly get up and see that the tunnel has collapsed around you. The entrance is blocked by crumbled stone. Your only hope is the small hole you've managed to blast in the ceiling. You climb up a pile of rubble and start chipping away.

"Help!" you cry, hoping someone will hear you. If they don't, you might be stuck here for a long time.

THE END

CONTINUED FROM PAGE 29.

"That's easy," you reply. "If I am the brother of the penguin next to me, and that penguin is not my brother, then the penguin must be my sister."

Sensei nods, smiling. "Well done," he says. "You are clever as well as brave. You both will make wonderful ninjas. We can begin your training immediately."

You and Amy high-five again. "All right!"

"There is one thing I must ask," Sensei says. "You must keep this training a secret from other penguins. I cannot train others until the Dojo is ready."

You and Amy nod solemnly. "We promise, Sensei," you say together.

Then you smile at each other. Your adventure in the mountains is over. But a new one is about to begin!

THE END

You walk slowly toward the black puffle.

"Hey there," you say. "How are you?"

The black puffle stops in its tracks. It turns and stares at you. You hold out your rucksack filled with O'berries. "How about a snack?"

Curious, the black puffle slowly hops toward you and sniffs the backpack. Then its eyes light up and it starts munching on the O'berries.

"Cool!" you say. "So, I'm going on an important quest. Want to come with me?"

The black puffle looks at you, intrigued.

"I'll pack lots of O'berries for our trip," you promise.

That seems to do the trick. The black puffle hops after you. You fill your rucksack with more O'berries and continue your journey.

Before long, you come to a mountain and see that the river flows underneath it. You walk into the mountain cave and are soon plunged into total darkness.

"Grub!" you cry. "I forgot to bring my flashlight."

Suddenly, a warm glow fills the passageway,

and you see that the black puffle is letting off a fiery flame.

"Thanks!" you say gratefully. With the black puffle lighting the way, you move on. As you get farther into the mountain, you hear the sound of rushing water ahead of you.

When you get closer, you realise that the river has widened into a huge whirlpool. There's no space to walk around it on your side of the river. You've got to get across. But how?

You look around the cave. Long stalactites are hanging down from the ceiling. You might be able to grab onto them and swing across.

There's also a jagged stalagmite on the other side of the whirlpool. You have a rope in your rucksack—if you lasso the rock on the other side, you could climb across using the rope.

If you swing on the stalactites, go to page 56.

If you use your rope, go to page 67.

CONTINUED FROM PAGES 11, 79.

You and Amy change into your climbing boots and begin your trek over the mountain. The path up the mountain is covered with snow, but it's not too steep and you're able to safely hike to the top.

"Whoa, look at that view," Amy says, gazing out across the snow-covered valley.

"It's beautiful," you agree. Then you nod toward a nearby boulder. "We should rest before we keep going."

"I'm pretty thirsty," Amy says, nodding.

You open your rucksack to get your water canteen and the haiku book that Sensei gave you spills out. It lands on the ground, open to a page. You read the haiku out loud.

> "The view from above
> Can reveal many new things.
> What is it you see?"

"Whoa, that's cool!" Amy says. "It's like a special message just for us!"

You gaze out into the distance. "The haiku seems to be saying that we'll see something important from up here," you add. "But what? I just see a lot of snow and more mountains."

There are three mountains across the frozen field, and they're all about the same height.

"Let's keep looking," Amy suggests. "Maybe we're missing something."

You look again. There's the hazy, orange sky. There are the three mountains. But wait a minute . . . two of the peaks are topped with snow, but the one in the middle isn't.

"Do you see that?" you ask, pointing.

"Yes," Amy says, nodding. "There's no snow on the mountain. And I think those clouds above it aren't clouds. I think they're smoke."

"It's a volcano!" the two of you say together.

"That's perfect!" you add. "A volcano has fire inside. It's surrounded by snow. That's fire and snow in one place."

"If there's water nearby, it will be the perfect spot for the Dojo," Amy adds.

"Let's go!" you cry.

You make your way down the mountain and head across the field. The ground is frozen solid, and your climbing boots help you walk on the frozen ground without sliding.

As you travel, you pass an old, abandoned building site littered with boards and a couple of ladders. A few minutes past the construction site, you notice the land is sloping up. The ground ahead looks uneven.

"Slow down, Amy," you say. "I think we need to be careful up here."

It's a good idea. You've come to a ravine, a deep crack in the ground. Looking down, you see that it's a long drop to the bottom and the ravine seems to stretch across the whole field. The only way to cross it is to jump over it.

"It's too risky to jump," you realise.

"We could throw a rope to the other side," Amy suggests.

"Or we could use those ladders from the building site," you say. "We could lay them across the ravine and climb over."

If you use the rope to get across the ravine, go to page 13.

If you go back to the building site and get the ladders, go to page 80.

CONTINUED FROM PAGE 46.

"I'll train with you," you reply. "Thank you, Sensei."

Over the next few weeks, Sensei teaches you all about the three elements. Then one day he approaches you.

"You are ready to continue your journey," he says. "Look at your map once more. The path you need to take is one you have not seen yet."

You study the map carefully, and you notice two things. One is a path that goes through the mountains. The other thing you notice is that the river looks like a path on the map. Maybe the river is the right way to go.

If you go to the river, go to page 31.

If you go to the mountains, go to page 69.

CONTINUED FROM PAGE 80.

"Let's keep going," you urge Amy, and she reluctantly agrees.

You slowly make your way across the field as the snow falls harder and harder. All you can make out is Amy's blue jacket, but at least you know she's next to you.

"We'd better be careful!" Amy calls over the roaring wind. "If we don't see the ravine, we might fall in!"

"Good point!" you yell back. You cover your eyes with your flipper, straining to see ahead.

You don't see the ravine—but you do see a soft, yellow light glowing in the distance. It moves closer and closer to you until finally you see the bearer of the light: Sensei!

"You should have taken shelter," he says gently. "I fear this path is too dangerous for you. Come, let me lead you back to Town."

Sensei safely leads you through the storm back to Town. In the end, you're grateful to be safe—but you wish you had taken shelter instead.

THE END

CONTINUED FROM PAGE 22.

You decide to let the black puffle choose for you. You hold out the book, the puffle hops on it, and it opens to a random page. You read the verse.

"Try and try again.
There is no shame in that path.
Why not start from scratch?"

You nod. "I guess we should go back to Sensei," you tell the black puffle. "After all, that's where we started."

Then you notice that the puffle is yawning.

"Would you like me to drop you off at my igloo?" you ask. "You could take a nap there."

The puffle nods gratefully, so you stop at your igloo on the way back to Sensei and leave it there. Then you find Sensei by the pond.

"Greetings, young penguin," he says. "What have you found?"

"A lot of water and snow," you say. "But no fire. I read a haiku from the book and it told me to start from scratch. So I came back here."

"That is very wise," Sensei says with a nod.

"And now I have another haiku for you."

He recites this verse:

> "The map holds secrets.
> Look carefully to find them.
> And trust what you see."

"So you're saying I should give the map another look?" you ask.

Sensei nods. "Sometimes, we miss the most important thing at first glance."

You study the map again. You notice the underground spring you saw before as well as a path through the mountains you didn't notice.

Hmm, you think. *Both of these are good choices. I wonder which one I should take?*

If you go to the underground spring, go to page 47.

If you go to the mountains, go to page 69.

CONTINUED FROM PAGE 62.

You realise that blowing up cream soda barrels in an underground tunnel could be dangerous. Trying to find the spot aboveground makes the most sense.

You make your way back to the Mine entrance, using one of the barrels to boost yourself up to the hole in the wall. Outside, you take out the map. You've got a strategy planned: You'll walk above the Mine, trying to imagine the tunnels underneath your flippers. It might not be exact, but it's the best chance you have of finding the spot.

It's nice to be out in the sunlight again, and you hum a tune as you walk along the snow. You've got the map right in front of you.

"Okay, so I make a right just about here," you mutter to yourself. "And then I keep going, oh, about one hundred paces."

You follow the path for a while. Then you look up. It looks like you're in the middle of nowhere. There's nothing but fields of snow all around you. You realise you have no idea where you are, or even how to get back to the Mine.

"Grub!" you say. "It's too bad I don't have a compass in my backpack."

Then you notice a figure coming toward you. It's Sensei! You run up to meet him.

"Boy, am I glad to see you!" you say. "I'm pretty sure there's a perfect spot for the Dojo around here somewhere. But I'm kind of lost."

"I may have sent you on this journey before you were ready," Sensei says in his soft, steady voice. "If you wish, I can give you some training to better prepare you. The choice is yours."

You wonder if this is some kind of test. If you accept Sensei's help, does that mean you're giving up?

If you accept Sensei's training, go to page 41.

If you decide to keep going without more training, go to page 49.

CONTINUED FROM PAGES 10, 44.

You decide to go to the underground spring. According to the map, it's underneath the Mine Shack. You say good-bye to Sensei and head there.

The Mine Shack is a rickety-looking building made of wood boards and painted red. A track for the mine carts emerges from the front of the building. You know that the tracks take the carts deep underneath Club Penguin.

A few small groups of penguins are hanging out outside the Mine Shack and talking.

"It's true," a red penguin says. "A friend of my friend's friend saw the ghost herself."

"My cousin saw it when she was playing *Cart Surfer*," a green penguin says. "It lives deep in the tunnels underneath the Mine Shack."

This rumour is just the kind of gossip you like. You're tempted to investigate, but you're on a mission for Sensei. You've got to stay focused.

You waddle to one of the mine carts and hop in, pulling a lever to set the cart rolling down the tracks. The cart slowly rolls into the dark Mine. Safety lights cast an eerie glow on the walls.

47

The map shows a tunnel leading to the underground spring that's not on the mine cart route. You carefully keep track of your journey, searching for the tunnel entrance.

Then you see it: a boarded-up tunnel in the wall on the right. You quickly pull the lever and the cart comes to a halt. Then you jump out and pry away the old boards so you can climb inside.

There's no light in here. You're wondering if you should go get a torch when you hear a noise up ahead.

You freeze. Was it just your imagination?

Creeeeeeeak!

Nope, that was a noise, all right. Is someone—or something—up there?

If you throw snowballs to scare whatever it is away, go to page 25.

If you sneak up on it, go to page 71.

CONTINUED FROM PAGE 46.

You decide to prove to Sensei that you can find the Dojo location on your own.

"I know I can find it," you say. "So, thank you, but I'll pass on the extra training."

Sensei nods. "The decision is yours."

You scan the snowy, white field. "It's got to be around here somewhere, I'm sure," you say. But when you look back at Sensei, he's gone. It's like he's vanished into thin air.

Feeling very alone, you start searching again for the spot above the underground hot spring. You're hoping to find some sign of a hot spring underneath—but everything looks the same. You check Sensei's haiku book to see what advice it holds.

> "The penguin who trains,
> Is not always the fastest.
> But is very wise."

It looks like you should have taken Sensei's offer after all!

THE END

CONTINUED FROM PAGE 32.

You find an empty boat tied up at the Dock. You hop aboard, turn on the motor, and head out into the sea.

Following the map, you steer the boat around the bottom of the island to the spot where the river meets the sea. As you explore the river, you glimpse groups of wild puffles happily playing in the wilderness. All the while, you keep your eyes open for some sign of a fire element.

Then you hear an unwelcome sound.

Putt . . . putt . . . putt . . . putt . . . putt . . .

It's the motor! You check the controls and realise that the fuel gauge reads *Empty*. You forgot to fuel up before you left the Dock!

The motor cuts out. You grab an emergency oar and try to paddle against the current. But the strong river carries you back where you came from—and pulls you out to sea.

You start paddling again, but you can't seem to get close to the shore. There's nothing to do but wait and hope that a rescue boat finds you soon.

THE END

CONTINUED FROM PAGE 79.

You and Amy decide to go around the mountain. As you waddle along, Amy asks you more questions about Sensei.

"I can't believe the rumours about ninjas are real," she says. "If that's true, who knows what else is on this island that we don't know about!"

Your mind starts to wander as you continue along the path, imagining what other secrets Club Penguin might hold.

Suddenly Amy stops. "Hey, look at that!"

She points off the trail to a set of very large footprints in the snow. The two of you leave the trail to investigate.

"They don't look like penguin prints," you remark. "They're wide and kind of round."

"Maybe they were penguin prints and the snow melted around them," Amy guesses.

You shake your head. "It's too cold up here for that. And the outline of the prints is very crisp. I think they belong to a large creature."

Amy's eyes grow wide. "Maybe it's a Yeti!" she says, her voice rising with excitement. "A penguin at the Pizza Parlor told me a rumour

51

that one lives in the mountains."

"You mean a big, hairy snow beast, like Bigfoot?" you ask.

"Exactly," Amy says. She reaches into her rucksack and whips out a camera. "We've got to find it and get a picture. I'm sure Aunt Arctic will print it in the newspaper!"

Getting proof of a Yeti is too good to pass up. "The tracks lead over there to that cave," you point out.

But before you can follow the tracks, you hear a strange, wild yowl coming from over the ridge. You and Amy look at each other.

"That could be the Yeti!" you cry.

If you go to the cave, go to page 57.

If you decide to climb a tree to look over the ridge, go to page 65.

CONTINUED FROM PAGE 80.

You and Amy arrange the old boards in the building site into a makeshift shelter. It's not much, but it protects you from the snow and wind. Amy builds a small fire, and the crackling flames keep you warm.

"What if we're stuck in this storm for a long time?" you wonder out loud.

You open up Sensei's haiku book to see what advice it has for you.

> "No path is easy,
> But you are close to your goal.
> Do not give up now."

"I like the sound of that," you say.

The storm passes after about an hour. You and Amy douse the fire with snow, and soon you're trekking across the snow, dragging the two ladders behind you. When you get to the ravine, you tie the ladders together with rope. Then you stand them up on your side of the ravine, and together you and Amy give them a push.

The ladders are long enough to reach the other side. Perfect!

"I'll go first," Amy says bravely. "Hold the ladders steady for me."

You grab on to the end of the ladders and watch as Amy begins a slow crawl across the ravine. To your relief, the ladders hold steady as Amy moves across. She reaches the other side, stands up and gives a triumphant whoop.

"Your turn!" she calls to you.

You squat down and begin to crawl over the ladders, just like Amy did. Then you catch a glimpse of the long drop below and your heart jumps into your throat.

"You can do it!" Amy encourages you.

Hearing the sound of your friend's voice gives you confidence. Before you know it, you're safely across the ravine. You and Amy head for the volcano.

When you reach the volcano, you stop.

"So we've got fire and snow here," you remind your friend. "Now we just have to find water."

"Let's climb up," Amy suggests. "Who knows what we'll find."

The sides of the volcano are steep, so you use the grappling hook and rope to scale the straight portions of the mountainside. Most of the time, you're able to climb up a rocky path.

You take a step on the path and your right flipper lands on a rock. Your boot slides off of your flipper and tumbles down the path, dropping onto a ledge at least ten feet below you.

"Grub!" you say. "I can't keep climbing without my boot."

You look down at the ledge. "It's a bit of a drop, but we can try it with the rope," you say.

"Maybe," Amy says, pointing. "But I see a path that goes down there. It's steep, but we should be able to do it."

If you drop down to the ledge to get your boot, go to page 23.

If you take the steep path, go to page 27.

"Hop up on my rucksack, and I'll carry you across," you tell the black puffle, but it takes one hop backward as if to say, "No way."

You jump up and grab the stalactite above you. Then you swing forward and grab the next one. You swing toward the third one, which hangs right above the centre of the whirlpool.

Crrrrrrack! You're too heavy for the spindly stalactite. It breaks off the ceiling, and you helplessly plummet into the whirlpool.

The water swirls around you, and some unseen force pulls you through a tunnel of water. You're terrified, but before panic can set in, you suddenly find yourself above water—and it's calm. You look around and realise you're in the Underground Pool!

Bewildered, you climb out of the pool and go to get the map out of your rucksack. The pocket is unzipped! The map is soaking wet and all of the ink has smeared. Without the map, your search is over.

THE END

CONTINUED FROM PAGE 52.

"Let's check out the cave," you suggest. "The footprints lead right to it."

"Sounds good to me," Amy agrees. "We should go quietly so the Yeti won't hear us."

The two of you quietly follow the footprints to the cave. As you get closer, you can see light smoke floating out into the open.

"The Yeti is inside!" Amy says with excitement. She holds her camera in front of her. "Let's rush in and get the photo."

You both run into the cave. You see a white figure bent over a fire . . .

Snap! Snap! Snap! Amy starts taking pictures. The white figure turns to face you . . .

"Oh, hello. Welcome to my cave. I'm Jim."

It's not a Yeti at all, but an orange penguin wearing a white coat and wide, round snowshoes.

"Hi." You introduce yourself and Amy. "Sorry to bother you. We saw strange footprints in the snow and thought they belonged to a Yeti. But I guess those were snowshoe prints."

Jim laughs. "Now that's funny. I've been exploring the wilderness of Club Penguin for a long time, but nobody's ever mistaken me for a Yeti before. Hey, do you want some tea?"

"That sounds great," you reply. You and Amy join Jim around the fire, sipping cups of strong tea. It reminds you of Sensei.

"This tea is delicious," you say. "My friend Sensei would really like this."

"I get the tea leaves from a special plant in the mountains," Jim says, handing you a small, cloth pouch. "Here, bring some to your friend."

"Thanks," you say. You stand up. "Amy and I need to get back to that path that goes around the mountain."

Jim shakes his head. "I hate to tell you this, but that path has been blocked by snow for months now. There's no way to get around."

"So what do we do now?" Amy asks.

"Let's bring the tea to Sensei and figure out what to do next," you suggest.

Go to page 11.

CONTINUED FROM PAGE 68.

The black puffle seems unsure of the idea, but it agrees to hop in your rucksack once more.

"Woo-hoo!" With a happy cry, you push off the riverbank and glide down the frozen ice. You're speeding along, glad you made this decision, when the ice underneath you suddenly gives way. Before you can jump to safety, you plunge into the icy water.

Luckily, you're a good swimmer. You swim back to shore, dodging floating sheets of ice, with the black puffle safely in your rucksack. As you climb back onto the ground you see a penguin coming toward you—it's Sensei!

He hands you a cup of steaming hot tea, which you accept gratefully.

"You have tried very hard to help me," he says. "But I fear this mission is too dangerous. My search for the Dojo will just have to wait."

You're disappointed, but you suspect Sensei is right. You're very lucky that you and the puffle got out of the ice safely!

THE END

CONTINUED FROM PAGE 29.

"Um, I'm not sure," you say. You glance at Amy, and she shrugs. "If the penguin isn't my brother, maybe he's my cousin?"

Sensei shakes his head. "You cannot be a brother to your cousin. But you can be a brother to your sister."

You slap your flipper on your forehead. "Grub! Of course!"

"You have both done so well," Sensei tells you. "Go and enjoy the many things to do on Club Penguin. When the Dojo is built, you will be ready."

"Thank you, Sensei," you and Amy say. Then you leave Sensei and head into Town.

It's too bad you got the riddle wrong, but you're not all that sad. At least you have a great story to tell your friends!

THE END

CONTINUED FROM PAGES 30, 72.

You decide to take the path to the right. Pia's torch lights the way as you move through the dark tunnel. Cobwebs hang from the ceiling, and you give a little shiver. Even though the ghost isn't real, the tunnel is still kind of spooky.

After you've travelled for a while, you realise you're feeling warm. The air feels hotter with each step you take. Then you hear a bubbling sound.

The path turns a corner, and you see a bubbling hot spring right in front of you! Steam rises from the water, filling the cavern. The water from the stream hangs from the ceiling in droplets and then slowly drips to the cavern floor. It's like an indoor rain forest.

"It's a place where water and fire meet!" you cry. That's two of the three elements you need for the Dojo location. All you need now is snow—but there isn't a flake to be seen inside this tunnel.

"Grub!" you say as a drop of water splashes on your forehead. You look up at the ceiling and then realise something. Above the tunnel, outside, is plenty of snow! That's a point where snow, water, and fire meet—but you have to get to the snow somehow.

You look at the map, thinking. You could go above ground, but it would be hard to find this spot again without following the tunnels. You need some kind of marker. Maybe you can poke a hole in the ceiling.

The ceiling is made of solid rock. You'd need to blast a hole through it somehow. You remember those cream soda barrels you saw back in the other part of the tunnel. They might be just what you need to make this happen.

If you blast a hole in the ceiling with cream soda barrels, go to page 33.

If you search aboveground instead, go to page 45.

CONTINUED FROM PAGE 22.

You close your eyes and open the book to a random page. Then you read the verse aloud.

> "Look one time and see.
> But one time is not enough.
> Look twice to see truth."

"I suppose it's saying I need to give things a second look to see the truth," you say. "I might as well give it a try."

You look at the waterfall again and the mountain peaks around it. But you don't see smoke or flames or anything that looks like fire.

> "Look twice to see the truth."

What are you missing? You look again. Snowy peak, waterfall, another peak, but this one has melting snow . . .

"That's it!" you cry, jumping up. The mountains around the waterfall are covered in snow. But one peak in front of the waterfall has no snow from the top to about halfway down. There has to be a reason the snow is melting. That mountain must be a dormant volcano!

What you thought were white clouds above it are actually plumes of smoke. That's got to be a volcano for sure. You've found snow, water and fire in one spot. It's the perfect place for Sensei's Dojo!

You can't wait to bring the news to Sensei. You carefully mark the spot on the map. Then you and the black puffle go back to Sensei and show him where the volcano is on the map.

"You have done well," Sensei says. "Please let me reward you."

He hands you a beautiful, handheld lantern made from gleaming copper.

"Thank you," you say. "Now I can light my way if I end up in the dark again."

The black puffle looks at you. Does this mean you won't need it anymore?

"Of course, nobody lights the way better than you," you tell your new friend. "How'd you like to be my pet?"

The puffle nods happily, and you feel great. Not only did you help Sensei, but you have a new puffle, too!

THE END

CONTINUED FROM PAGE 52.

Amy puts her camera strap over her neck and quickly climbs a tree so she can get a better look at the ridge. A few minutes later she climbs down.

"I got it!" she says excitedly. "I saw a big, white, furry creature! I'm sure it was the Yeti. And now I've got proof!"

"This is amazing," you say. "We need to get this to Aunt Arctic right away."

You head back to Town as quickly as you can. You find Aunt Arctic in the Coffee Shop. She is wearing a pink cap and glasses. She's busy typing on a laptop.

"Aunt Arctic, have we got a photo for you!" Amy says. "We spotted a real Yeti in the mountains!"

"How exciting," Aunt Arctic says. "Let's take a look."

Amy hooks up her camera to the laptop and downloads the photo. You lean in to see it, holding your breath.

It's a photo of a big, white *something*—but it's very blurry.

"Oh no," Amy says sadly. "He must have moved when I took the photo. Sorry, Aunt Arctic."

"No need to apologize," Aunt Arctic says. "This photo is very intriguing, even if it is blurry. I'll be happy to publish it in the next issue of *The Club Penguin Times*. I hope you'll write a story to go along with it."

"Of course we will," Amy says.

Then you remember. "But what about Sensei?" you say. "We've got to get back on the path."

"That's right!" Amy says. "You should show Aunt Arctic the map."

You take the map out of your backpack—and the image has faded! In its place is a haiku.

"To start is easy.
But you must stick to your goal,
Or you won't finish."

You sigh. "I guess we won't be able to find the Dojo location now," you say.

"Yeah," Amy says. "But at least we're going to be in *The Club Penguin Times*."

THE END

The stalactites hanging from the ceiling don't look strong enough to support the weight of you and your rucksack. You decide that the rope is the best way to get across.

You take the rope from your pack and tie the end into a lasso using a special knot. You twirl the rope over your head three times and then throw it over the whirlpool.

The end of the rope loops over the stalagmite growing up from the ground. Perfect! You pull the rope to tighten the loop. Then you tie the rope to a rock on your side of the whirlpool.

You unzip your rucksack. "Hop in and I'll take you across," you tell the black puffle.

Your new friend eagerly jumps inside. You grab the rope and pull yourself across the whirlpool, flipper over flipper. When you reach the other side, you gratefully flop onto the rocky floor of the cavern.

"Whew! I'm glad we didn't fall in," you say. The black puffle jumps out of your rucksack and nods in agreement. You pull the rope off

the rocks and put it back in your pack. Then
you and the puffle continue to head through the
mountain.

You follow the river for another hour before
you come to the other side of the mountain—
and the exit. But there's one problem: It's
blocked with a wall of snow. The river seems to
be flowing underneath the frozen exit.

"I guess we could swim underneath it,"
you say with a frown, but the black puffle has it
covered. The puffle flames up again and melts
a hole in the snow that's big enough for both of
you to crawl through.

You emerge into the bright sunlight. It feels
much colder out here and as you walk you notice
that the river seems to be frozen solid.

"Hmm," you say. "We could probably save
time if we slide on the ice."

**If you stay on the riverbank,
go to page 21.**

If you slide on the ice, go to page 59.

CONTINUED FROM PAGES 41, 44.

"Sensei, I've made my decision," you call out.

Sensei walks toward you. "What is your choice?"

"I'm going to the mountains," you reply. "I noticed something that I missed before."

Sensei nods. "I believe you have made a wise choice. Keep your eyes open, and remember what you have learned."

It's a long trek to the mountains, so you check your gear to make sure you have everything you need. Some mountain climbing gear might be useful. You head to the Gift Shop to stock up before you go.

The Gift Shop is filled with everything from hats to fancy clothes to adventure gear. You're checking out a grappling hook and a pair of climbing boots when you hear a voice behind you.

"Are you going climbing without me?"

You turn and see your friend Amy, a blue penguin wearing boots, a warm coat and a winter hat. You and Amy have spent many hours exploring Club Penguin together. She's been following the ninja rumours, too.

You decide to tell her what's been going on.

"You won't believe this, but I met a ninja master in the wilderness!" you say.

Amy's eyes get wide. "No way! What does he look like? Where is he? Can I meet him?"

You quickly tell Amy your story. "So now I'm headed to the mountains," you finish. "I think what I'm searching for might be there."

"I am *so* coming with you," Amy says. "I'll help. And you know that mountain climbing is safest when you're with a buddy."

"You're right," you say. "But Sensei selected me for this quest personally. I'm not sure if I'm allowed to let anyone help me."

If you continue on your quest without Amy, go to page 19.

If you let Amy come with you, go to page 76.

CONTINUED FROM PAGE 48.

You slowly make your way toward the noise, step by step. As your eyes adjust to the darkness, you make out a shape in front of you. It's all white . . . could it be the ghost?

Your heart pounds as you get closer to the mysterious figure.

"Who's there?" the ghost asks. But it sounds more like a penguin than a ghost.

"Why don't you tell me?" you reply. You're close to the *ghost* now, and you see the truth— it's not a ghost at all. "Hey, wait. Are you wearing a sheet?"

"You got me," she says, removing her sheet. "My name's Pia. I decided to play a prank on my friends, so I started a rumour about a ghost in the Mine and then put on this disguise."

"You're doing a good job," you say. "Everyone is talking about the ghost."

Pia's face brightens. "Really? That's cool. Maybe I'll leave now. It's kind of spooky in here."

"No kidding," you agree. "I'm looking for something down here, but it's hard without a torch."

"No problem," Pia says. "You can have mine."

"Thanks!" you say happily. You shine the torch around the tunnel.

"I'm supposed to go that way, but it looks like a dead end," you remark.

Curious, Pia follows you to the end of the tunnel. It's a wall of rock, but there's a penguin-sized hole just above your head that must lead to the other side of the tunnel.

"Can you please give me a boost?" you ask Pia.

"Sure!" she replies, and soon you're tumbling through the hole. You land with a thump on the Mine floor. You've landed in some kind of old storage room. Cream soda barrels are piled up against the walls.

You thank Pia and shine the torch ahead of you. The tunnel forks in two directions. You look at the map, but the fork isn't there. You're not sure which way to go.

If you go left, go to page 30.
If you go right, go to page 61.

CONTINUED FROM PAGE 26.

"I'm in," you tell Pia. "What are we going to do?"

Minutes later, you start your prank.

"Whoooo . . . whoooo . . . whoooo!"

The penguins turn toward the Mine entrance and see a ghost floating out of the Mine. It's white and sways back and forth spookily.

"It's the ghost!" someone yells.

The frightened penguins run away. You and Pia emerge from the Mine, laughing. You draped the sheet over a rope and you and Pia moved it back and forth. Then you made ghost noises. It worked great!

"That was fun," you say. "But now I've got to get back to my quest."

You look for the map in your rucksack, but it's gone! Pia helps you search the Mine, but you can't find it anywhere.

You're disappointed that you can't finish your quest, but at least you made a friend. You and Pia head off to play a game of *Mancala*.

THE END

CONTINUED FROM PAGE 16.

If you make friends with the black puffle, it might take time away from your quest. You decide to keep going.

Up ahead, the river flows underneath a pass that cuts right through a mountain. You check the map and realise that you have no choice but to follow the river inside.

It's dark inside the mountain, and the farther you go, the darker it gets.

"I should have brought a torch," you mutter. It's difficult to see more than a few feet in front of you.

Then you take a step and, instead of touching down on rock, your flipper hits water. Startled, you plunge into the icy cold river. You can feel the strong pull of the water as it swirls and swirls around you. You've accidentally stepped into a whirlpool!

"Heeeeelp!" you cry, but there's no one around to hear you. You're a good swimmer, but you can't resist the pull of the whirlpool. The strong, swirling water pulls you under . . .

The next thing you know, you can feel that

you're on dry land. You open your eyes and see Sensei looking down at you.

"Where am I?" you ask, sitting up.

"In the wilderness," Sensei says, and you can see that you're back at the reflective pond.

"How did I get here?" you ask.

"That is not important," Sensei says. "You have done well. But you need to strengthen your fire skills. I cannot allow you to continue."

You frown. "Grub! I'm sorry I let you down. I really want to learn how to be a ninja."

"There is another way you can help," Sensei says. "The Dojo will need gongs. I can teach you how to smelt metal and make them. You will strengthen your fire skills that way."

"Yes!" you say without hesitating.

Sensei waddles over to a wood chest and comes back with a dark, leather apron. "You will need this Goldsmith Apron."

"Thanks, Sensei," you say. You're sorry you didn't find the Dojo location, but making gongs out of metal sounds like a lot of fun—and you still get to help Sensei.

THE END

CONTINUED FROM PAGE 70.

Before you make your decision, you think about what Sensei told you: to remember what you had learned so far. The very first haiku you read sticks in your head:

> "Alone you travel.
> But when a friend offers help,
> Do not refuse her."

The choice seems clear. "Of course you can come, Amy. I don't think I'm supposed to do this alone."

Amy grins. "Hooray!"

You nod to the mountain climbing gear on the wall. "We'd better stock up before we go."

"Right," Amy agrees. "Where exactly are we going, anyway?"

You take the map out of your rucksack and show her. "We're taking a path through the mountains. We need to find a place where water, snow and fire meet."

"Hmm," Amy says. "That could be a challenge. The grappling hook and boots are good for climbing. But it looks like there are a lot of snowy hills out there. Sleds or skis would make getting over them much faster."

"How about the sleds?" you suggest. "I think they'll be easier to carry than the skis. Besides, I'm great at *Sled Racing*."

"Yeah, but I beat you last time!" Amy teases. "Let's get them."

Soon you're heading away from the Gift Shop toward the mountains of Club Penguin. You and Amy are both dragging sleds behind you.

It's easy going at first. You and Amy talk as you hike along. Before you know it, you've reached the mountains.

It's colder here, and you're glad that you're wearing warm coats. There are no other penguins in sight anywhere.

"It's kind of lonely out here," Amy remarks.

You nod. "And quiet, too."

You stop walking and cup your flippers around your beak. "Helloooooooo!" you call out loudly. "Is anyone out there?"

Your voice echoes off the mountains.

Out there? . . . out there? . . . out there? . . .

"That's so cool!" Amy cries. "Let me try. Helloooooooooo!"

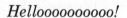

Helloooooooooo!

"Let's try it together," you suggest.

"Helloooooooo out there!" you both yell.

You wait for the echo, but it doesn't come. Instead, a loud, rumbling sound like thunder fills the valley. But there's no storm brewing. It's something much more dangerous.

Amy points at the mountain peak to the left of you. A wall of snow is sliding down the mountain at rapid speed.

"It's an avalanche!" she cries.

Within seconds, a massive wave of snow will be upon both of you. You spot a cave in the mountainside and start to run toward it.

"Not there!" Amy cries out. "The snow will trap us inside."

You stop, realising she's right.

"The sleds!" Amy cries as the snow rushes closer. "We've got to ride the wave!"

You get your sled in front of you just as the snow roars past you. Instead of letting it knock you over, you hop belly first on your sled and leap onto the wave.

"Wooo-hooooo!" The island goes past you in a blur as you zoom across the frozen wave, travelling faster than you ever have before. When the avalanche finally stops, it pushes you forward and you tumble off your sled and into the snow. But you're safe.

"Amy?" you call out, jumping to your feet.

Amy waddles up, pulling her sled. "Right here," she says. "That was scary—but awesome!"

"Definitely," you agree. You pull out your map. "Let's see where we are."

You're not too far off the path, which goes across a very wide mountain just up ahead. You show the map to Amy.

"It will take a long time to go around," you say. "Maybe we should try climbing over it. We've got the gear."

If you climb the mountain, go to page 38.

If you go around the mountain, go to page 51.

"I think the ladders might be safer," you say. "Let's go back and get them."

As you walk back to the site, you notice that pale, grey clouds are quickly sweeping across the sky. The air suddenly feels colder, and a wind is whipping up.

Amy looks up and frowns. "Looks like a storm is coming."

Snow is starting to fall as you grab two ladders and head back to the ravine. It starts slowly, but soon it's coming down in sheets. You can barely see in front of you.

"What should we do?" Amy asks. "It's getting dangerous out here."

You know Amy's right, but you're so close to your goal! You don't want to give up now.

If you keep going, go to page 42.

If you find shelter from the storm, go to page 53.